# Alien & Possum

## Friends No Matter What

by **Tony Johnston**

pictures by **Tony DiTerlizzi**

Aladdin Paperbacks

New York   London   Toronto   Sydney   Singapore

*For Kevin,*
*dear, sweet possum of an editor.*
*And for all the possums who have landed*
*in my trash can.*
—T. J.

*To the memory of Arnold Lobel—May your words and pictures*
*hop into many a young mind for years to come.*
—T. D.

First Aladdin Paperbacks edition September 2002
Text copyright © 2001 by Tony Johnston
Illustrations copyright © 2001 by Tony DiTerlizzi

ALADDIN PAPERBACKS
An imprint of Simon & Schuster Children's Publishing Division
1230 Avenue of the Americas, New York, NY 10020

Book design by Anahid Hamparian
The text of this book was set in 20-point Bembo.
The illustrations are rendered on Strathmore plate bristol board, in "Winsor and Alien" brand watercolors
and gouache along with "Possum Prismacolors" colored pencils.
Printed in Mexico
2  4  6  8  10  9  7  5  3  1

Also available in a Simon and Schuster Books for Young Readers hardcover edition.
The Library of Congress has cataloged the hardcover edition as follows:
Johnston, Tony, 1942–
Alien and Possum: friends no matter what/by Tony Johnston; illustrated by Tony DiTerlizzi.
p. cm. Summary: Possum and Alien become friends and find that they have both
similarities and differences.
ISBN 0-689-83835-2 (hc)
[1. Opossums-Fiction. 2. Extraterrestrial beings-Fiction.
3. Friendship-Fiction.] I. DiTerlizzi, Tony, ill. II. Title.
PZ7.J6478Al  2001 [E]-dc21  00-045065

ISBN  0-689-85326-2 (Aladdin pbk.)

# Contents

# Alien

Possum loved to stay up late. One night he was outside enjoying the stars.

A star fell. No, it was a spaceship.

"Oooh," said Possum. He looked close.

4

*Dit-dit-dit.* A space creature came out.
It was made of many strange things.

It made many strange sounds.
*Wreench. Creench. Cronk.*

Possum made a strange sound too.
"OOOOOOH!" said Possum.

The space creature got scared.
*WREENCH! CREENCH! CRONK!*
It screeched.

Then it ran away. *Dit-dit-dit-dit-dit.*

"Stop!" cried Possum. He ran after it.

It did not stop. *Dit-dit-dit-dit-dit-dit-dit.*
It ran faster.

It ran among the trees.

It ran behind a tree and hid.

"Where are you?" called Possum.

"I am far away," said a close voice.

"Are you here?" asked Possum.

"No, I am not here," said the voice.
"I am gone."

"That is too bad," Possum said. "If you
were here, I would be your friend."

11

"What is a friend?" asked
the voice.

Possum said, "Someone who
likes you no matter what."

"But we are not the same,"
said the voice. "You make
strange sounds.
I do not."

"What strange sounds do I make?" asked Possum.

"Strange sounds that go 'OOOOOOH!'" said the voice.

"Anyone can be friends," Possum said.

"You are hairy. I am smooth,"
said the voice.

"We can still be friends,"
Possum said.

"I am many colors,"
said the voice.
"You are no color at all."

"I am gray," said Possum,
"the color of a rain cloud.
Things of all colors can be friends."

"Goody!" cried the voice.

*Dit-dit-dit.* The space creature came out
from behind the tree.

"I am Alien," it said.

Possum said, "I am Possum."

Alien walked up to Possum and hugged
him. Possum hugged Alien back.

"We are friends," they said together,
"no matter what."

Then Possum said, "Alien?"

"Yes, Possum?"

"You make strange sounds too."

*Wreench. Creench. Cronk.* Alien laughed.

Then they went home to
Possum's tree.

# The Trash Can

One night, Possum was hungry.

He said, "I need a snack, Alien. Let's find some trash."

"What is trash?" Alien asked.

"Trash is something delicious," said Possum.

"Like high voltage?" asked Alien.

Possum groaned. "No, Alien. Like potato skins. And cold oatmeal. And old fish heads. This is what delicious is."

"Oh," Alien said.

Possum led the way.

*Dit-dit-dit.* Alien followed.

Sometimes they looked for falling stars.
Or the moon.

Mostly they looked for trash.

All the time Possum sniffed.

"You are making strange sounds,
Possum," said Alien.

"I am not," Possum said.
"I am sniffing."

"Sniffing sounds silly," said Alien.

Possum said, "Sniffing is the most unsilly thing there is, Alien. Sniffing helps me find trash."

"Oh," said Alien.

Sniffing helped Possum find trash.

Soon Possum was nose-to-nose
with a trash can.

"Goody!" cried Possum. "Trash!"

"Goody!" cried Alien for no reason.

Then Possum said, "Alien, please
help me tip the trash can."

"I would love to," said Alien.

*Dit-dit-dit.* Alien pushed. The trash
can toppled.

"Thank you, Alien," Possum said.
He began to nibble trash.

Alien did not nibble trash. It did not
nibble anything. It looked at the trash
can. It liked the trash can.

"Hello," said Alien.

The trash can said nothing.

*"Hello,"* said Alien.

The trash can said nothing.

"HELLO!" shouted Alien.

The trash can did not say a word.

*DIT!* Alien bumped it. Alien gave it a big dent.

The trash can was quiet.

Alien was loud.

*DIT-DIT-DIT-DIT-DIT!* Alien bumped the trash can many times. Alien gave it many dents.

"It is too loud to eat!" shouted Possum. "What is the matter?"

Alien said, "This trash can will not say 'hello.'"

"Alien," said Possum, "trash cans don't talk."

"Oh," Alien said.

Alien sniffed very loudly.
Then it walked away. *Dit-dit-dit.*

Possum was not hungry anymore.
So he followed Alien home.

# The Bedtime Story

It was late at night.

Possum was in bed.
He was reading a book.
He was crying.

His tears were falling
on the pages.

"Why are you crying?"
asked Alien.

"I am reading a bedtime
story," Possum said.

Alien said, "It must be sad."

"Very sad," Possum said. "It is the
saddest bedtime story I know."

"Why?" Alien asked.

"Because it makes me droopy," answered Possum. "It makes me drowsy. It makes me fall asleep."

"But Possum," said Alien, "aren't bedtime stories for falling asleep?"

"Not at the beginning!" cried Possum. "I always fall asleep too soon. I never know the end."

"Then give me the bedtime story," said Alien. "I will read it to you. Maybe that will keep you awake."

"Okay, Alien," Possum said. "Read the bedtime story to me. But if I fall asleep, please pinch me."

"Okay, Possum," Alien said. "I will be glad to pinch you. But what if you still sleep?"

"If I still sleep, please put ice down my pajamas," Possum said.

"Okay, Possum," Alien said. "I will be glad to put ice down your pajamas. But what if you *still* sleep?"

"Then, let me sleep," said Possum.

The bedtime story was soggy with tears.

Alien read it anyway.

Possum listened.
He drooped.

He drowsed.
He fell asleep.

"Wake up, Possum!" said Alien.
"You are missing the bedtime story!"

But Possum went on sleeping.

So Alien pinched Possum.

Possum went on sleeping.

So Alien put ice down Possum's pajamas.

Possum went on sleeping.

So Alien let him sleep.

Possum woke much later. He cried, "I missed the end again!"

Alien said, "I tried hard to keep you awake."

"Did you pinch me?" asked Possum.

"Yes, I did," said Alien.

"Did you put ice down my pajamas?" asked Possum.

"Yes, I did," said Alien. "Then I let you sleep."

"Why did you do that?" Possum screamed.

"You told me to," said Alien.

"Then read it to me now," said Possum. "I am wide awake."

"I cannot read it to you now," said Alien. "The book is gone. It was such a good bedtime story I ate it."

"Oh." Possum drooped like a wilted flower.

"Don't be sad," Alien said. "I know the whole bedtime story."

"You do?" asked Possum.

"Of course," said Alien. "I have an electro-perfect memory. And I did not fall asleep."

"Will you tell it to me now?" asked Possum. "While I am wide awake?"

"Of course I will," said Alien.

"Goody," said Possum.

So Alien told Possum the bedtime
story in the daytime. In the sun.
And Possum did not fall asleep.
He heard it to the very end.